Tiggers Hate to Lose

Disney's
Winnie the Pooh First Readers

Disney's

A Winnie the Pooh First Reader

Tiggers Hate to Lose

Isabel Gaines

ILLUSTRATED BY Francesc Rigol

DISNEY
PRESS

NEW YORK

Tiggers Hate to Lose

One fine spring day,

while bouncing beside the stream,

Tigger found Pooh and his friends

standing on the bridge.

They were all staring into the water.

"What are you doing?" Tigger asked.

"We're playing Pooh Sticks," said Pooh.

"Tiggers love Pooh Sticks!" said Tigger.

"What's Pooh Sticks?"

"It's a game," said Pooh.

"Get some sticks,

and you can play, too."

Tigger found some sticks

and bounced back to the bridge.

"The first stick to pass

under the bridge wins,"

explained Rabbit.

"On your mark, get set . . . go!"

Pooh, Piglet, Rabbit,
Roo, and Eeyore
threw their sticks
into the water.

Tigger decided to watch once
before trying it himself.

Then they all raced

to the other side

of the bridge

to see who won.

"I can see mine!" Roo shouted.

"I win!"

But just as he said the words,

Roo's "stick" spread its wings

and flew up

to join the other dragonflies.

"Can you see yours, Pooh?" Piglet asked.

"No," Pooh replied.

"I expect my stick is stuck."

"Look," Rabbit cried.

"There's Eeyore's stick!"

"Oh, joy," muttered Eeyore.

"I won."

17

"Step aside," Tigger said.

"Tiggers are great at Pooh Sticks."

Everyone moved over

so Tigger could play, too.

Once again, Rabbit gave the signal,

"On your mark, get set . . . go!"

19

They tossed their sticks

off the bridge . . .

. . . then raced to the other side.

Tigger shouted, "Did I win?"

"Nope," mumbled Eeyore. "I did."

"Oh," said Tigger, frowning.

"Well, I was just warming up.

Let's play again."

They played again,

and just like before,

Eeyore's stick sailed past the others.

"Tiggers don't like losing,"

grumbled Tigger.

"Let's play again."

Eeyore won the next game, too.

"Ooo, goody," Eeyore said.

"I've won four times in a row."

25

Eeyore won the next time,

and the next time,

and the time after that, too.

"I just can't lose," muttered Eeyore.

Tigger stamped his foot.

"Let's play again," he said.

"Tiggers *hate* to lose."

During the next game,

at the very last moment,

Eeyore's stick

squeaked by Tigger's.

Tigger threw down his sticks.

"Tiggers don't like Pooh Sticks!"

he cried.

Tigger walked away
with his head down
and no bounce at all.

"I'll tell you my secret,"

Eeyore called.

"You have to drop your stick

in a twitchy sort of way."

31

Tigger bounced back
to the bridge.
This time when he
dropped his stick,
Tigger made sure to twitch.

And this time,

Tigger's stick won!

Tigger was so happy,

he began bouncing again.

33

And he bounced right into Eeyore.

Can you match the words with the pictures?

stick

bridge

dragonfly

Tigger

Eeyore

Fill in the missing letters.

_ater

R_bbit

Pig_et

th_ew

foo_

Join the Pooh Friendship Club!

A wonder-filled year of friendly
activities and interactive fun for your child!

The fun starts with:
- Clubhouse play kit
- Exclusive club T-shirt
- The first issue of "Pooh News"
- Toys, stickers and gifts
  from Pooh

The fun goes on with:

- Quarterly issues of "Pooh News" each
  with special surprises
- Birthday and Friendship Day cards
  from Pooh
- And more!

Join now and also get a colorful, collectible Pooh art print

Yearly membership costs just $25
plus 15 Hunny Pot Points.
(Look for Hunny Pot Points 3
on Pooh products.)

To join, send check or money order and
Hunny Pot Points to:

Pooh Friendship Club
P.O. Box 1723
Minneapolis, MN 55440-1723

Please include the following information:
Parent name, child name, complete address,
phone number, sex (M/F), child's birthday,
and child's T-shirt size (S, M, L)
(CA and MN residents add applicable sales tax.)

Call toll-free for more information
1-888-FRNDCLB

Kit materials not intended for children under 3 years of age. Kit
materials subject to change without notice. Please allow 8-10 weeks for
delivery. Offer expires 6/30/99. Offer good while supplies last. Please do
not send cash. Void where restricted or prohibited by law. Quantities may
be limited. Disney is not liable for correspondence, requests, or orders
delayed, illegible, lost or stolen in the mail. Offer valid in the U.S. and
Canada only. ©Disney. Based on the "Winnie the Pooh" works, copyright
A.A. Milne and E.H. Shepard.

Fun
for kids
ages 3-8!

Poo

Wonderfully Whimsical Ways To Bring Winnie The Pooh Into Your Child's Life.

Pooh FRIENDSHIP

Pooh and the gang help children learn about liking each other for who they are in 5 charming volumes about what it means to be a friend.

Pooh STORYBOOK CLASSICS

Pooh PLAYTIME

Pooh LEARNING

These 4 enchanting volumes let you share the original A.A. Milne stories — first shown in theaters — you so fondly remember from your own childhood.

Children can't help but play and pretend with Pooh and his friends in 5 playful volumes that celebrate the joys of being young.

Pooh and his pals help children discover sharing and caring in 5 loving volumes about growing up.

FREE*
Flash Cards Attached!
A Different Set With Each *Pooh Learning* Video!
* With purchase, while supplies last.

Printed in U.S.A. © Disney Enterprises, Inc.